A NOTE TO PARENTS

One of the most important ways children learn to read — and learn to *like* reading — is by being with readers. Every time you read aloud, read along, or listen to your child read, you are providing the support that she or he needs as an emerging reader.

Disney's First Readers were created to make that reading time fun for you and your child. Each book in this series features characters that most children already recognize from popular Disney films. The familiarity and appeal of these high-interest characters will draw emerging readers easily into the story and at the same time support basic literacy skills, such as understanding that print has meaning, connecting oral language to written language, and developing cueing systems. And because Disney's First Readers are highly visual, children have another tool to help in understanding the text. This makes early reading a comfortable, confident experience — exactly what emerging readers need to become successful, fluent readers.

Read to Your Child

Here are a few hints to make early reading enjoyable and educational:

★ Talk with children before reading. Let them see how much they already know about the Disney characters. If they are unfamiliar with the movie basis of a book, take a few minutes to look at the cover and some of the illustrations to establish a context. Talking is important, since oral language precedes and supports reading.

★ Run your finger along the text to show that the words carry the story. Let your child read along if she or he recognizes that there are repeated words or phrases.

★ Encourage questions. A child's questions are good clues to his or her comprehension or thinking strategies.

★ Be prepared to read the same book several times. Children will develop ease with the story and concepts, so that later they can concentrate on reading and language.

Let Your Child Read to You

You are your child's best audience, so encourage her or him to read aloud to you often. And:

★ If children ask about an unknown word, give it to them. Don't interrupt the flow of reading to have them sound it out. However, if children start to sound out a word, let them.

★ Praise all reading efforts warmly and often!

—Patricia Koppman
Past President
International Reading Association

For my father
— J. K.

Paints and pencils by Sol Studios

ISBN 0-590-39384-7

12 11 10 9 8 7 6 5 4 3 2 1   8 9/9 0 1 2 3/0
Printed in the U.S.A.   23
First Scholastic printing, January 1998

BUZZ AND THE BUBBLE PLANET

by Judy Katschke
Illustrated by Sol Studios

Disney's First Readers — Level 3
A Story from Disney's *Toy Story*

SCHOLASTIC INC.
New York Toronto London Auckland Sydney

A new toy in Andy's room could mean fun—
or it could mean trouble!
"What *is* that thing?" the other toys asked.
"It looks like a spaceship!" Woody said.
Buzz Lightyear hopped off Andy's bed.
"Did someone say 'spaceship'?" he asked.

"Be careful, Buzz," Woody warned. "You're not real. You're a toy!"

"So is this spaceship," Buzz said. "It's a match made in heaven!"

"I think it was made in Japan," Hamm said.

Buzz climbed into the cockpit.

"I'm taking this baby for a test run!" he cried.

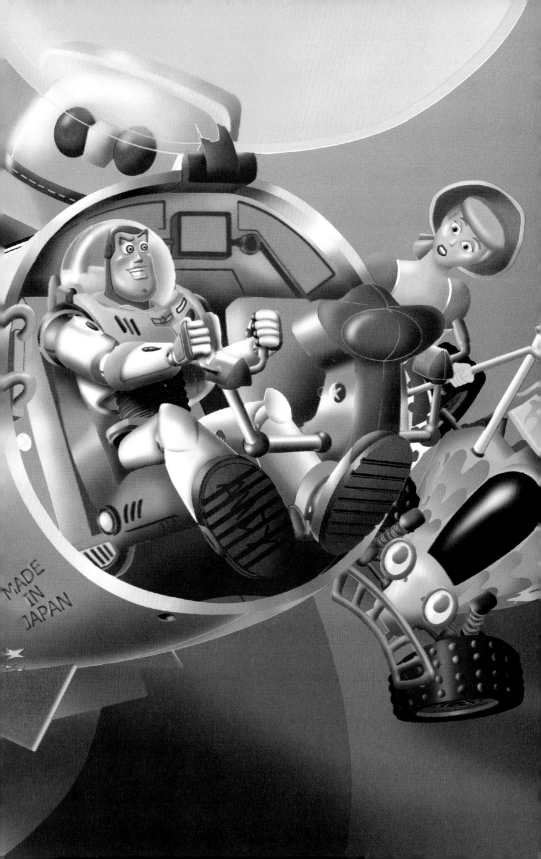

"I want to help," Hamm said.
Hamm took a piece of paper from the box.
"Quit hogging the instructions, Hamm," Bo Peep said.
"I don't need instructions!" Buzz cried.
Woody grabbed the spaceship.
"Buzz, this is a bad idea!" he cried.
But Woody goofed. He hit the on switch by mistake!

The spaceship began to bounce and shake.

"Ready for liftoff!" Buzz shouted.

WHOOSH! The ship blasted out the door . . . and out of sight!

The spaceship soared through the air. Buzz couldn't control it. It began to fall!

"Oh, no!" cried Buzz. "I'm going to crash!"

The ship fell from the sky. Buzz went flying out. . . .

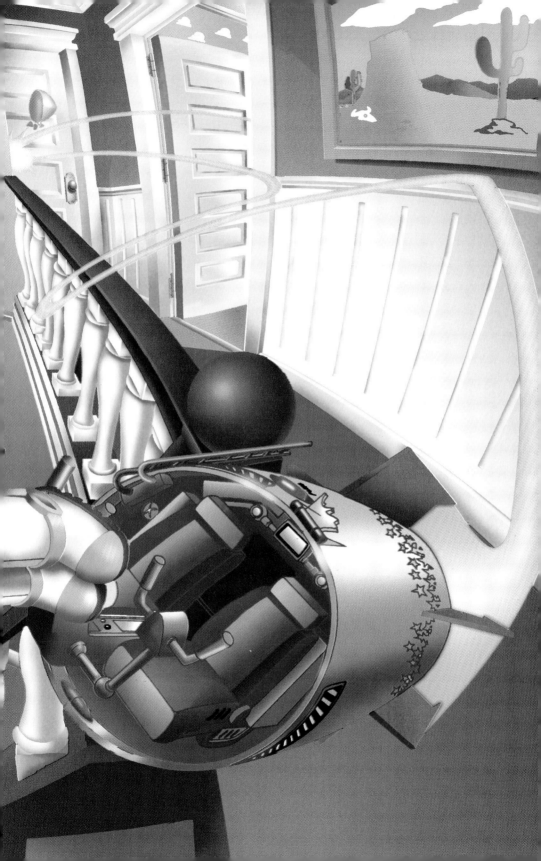

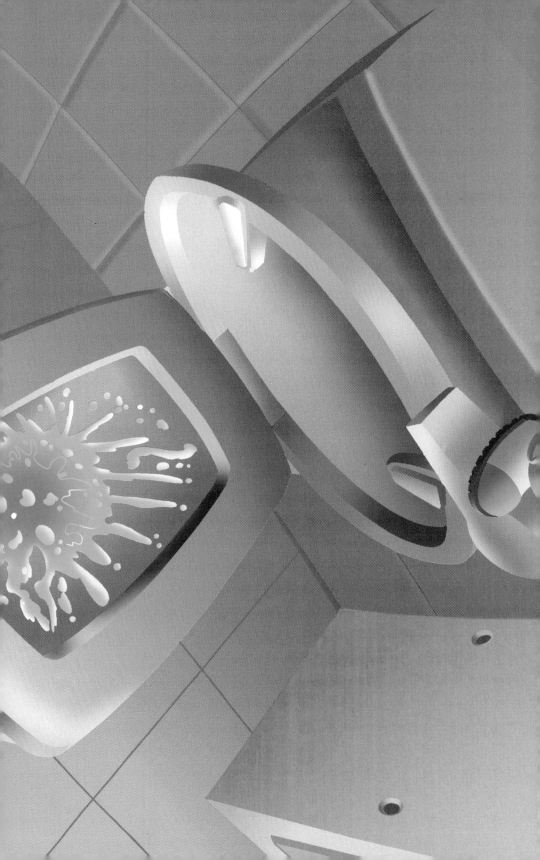

. . . and splash-landed inside a deep crater full of water.

Buzz was not hurt. He slowly peeked out and looked around.

"I seem to have crash-landed on a strange planet!" Buzz said.

He jumped out of the crater. Suddenly, the water was sucked into a hole.

"Now that's what I call infinity and beyond!" Buzz said.

Buzz felt like he was light-years away from Andy's room.

How will I get back home without my spaceship? he wondered.

Buzz decided to make the best of it. He would explore this strange planet.

"I may be a toy," Buzz said, "but I'm still Buzz Lightyear, space ranger!"

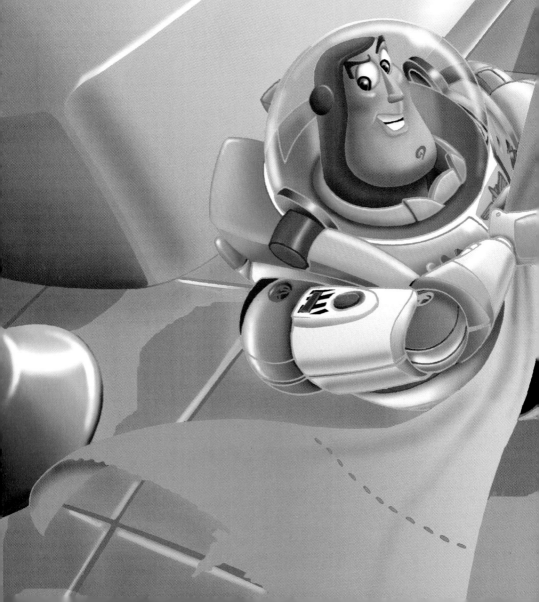

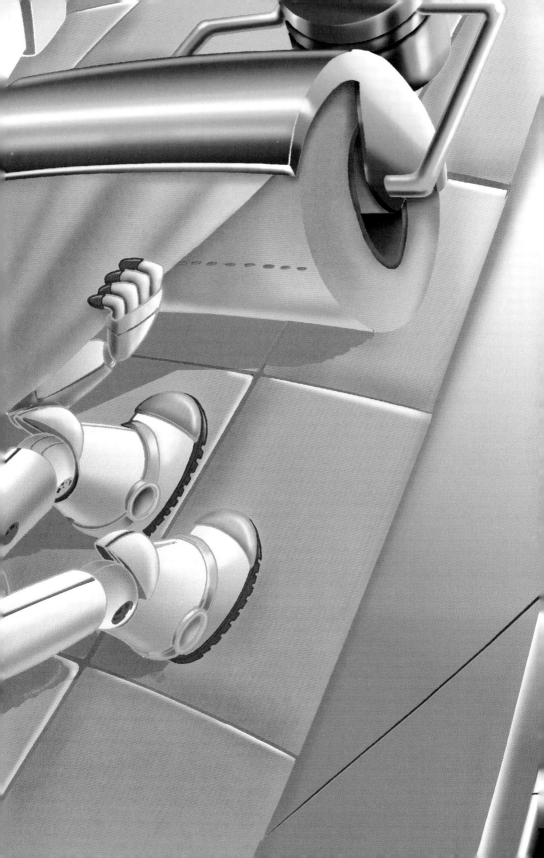

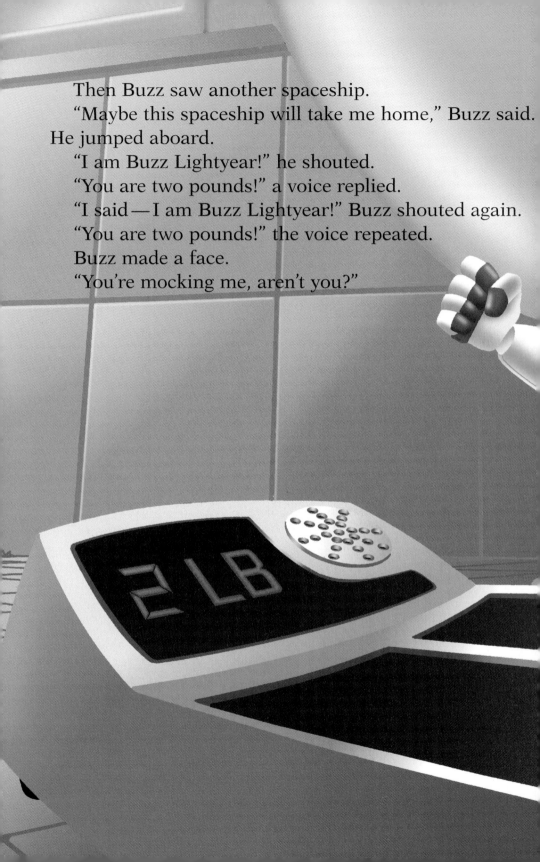

Then Buzz saw another spaceship.

"Maybe this spaceship will take me home," Buzz said. He jumped aboard.

"I am Buzz Lightyear!" he shouted.

"You are two pounds!" a voice replied.

"I said—I am Buzz Lightyear!" Buzz shouted again.

"You are two pounds!" the voice repeated.

Buzz made a face.

"You're mocking me, aren't you?"

Back in Andy's room, the toys held a meeting.

"How will we find Buzz?" Woody asked.

"Don't ask me," Bo Peep said. "I'm still trying to find my sheep!"

"I'll send out the troops!" Sarge said.

Woody smiled. "That's a great idea, Sarge!"

Sarge called the troops. "Fall in, soldiers!" he shouted.

"I wish I could roar like that," Rex sighed.

Meanwhile, Buzz was wrestling a strange robot. It had a long neck and a fuzzy face.

The robot shook. The robot whirred. It tickled Buzz all over!

Buzz pressed a yellow dot on the robot's neck. The robot stopped moving.

"Whew!" Buzz said. "That was a close brush with danger!"

Buzz's brush with the robot had him all shook-up.
But he didn't give up. He kept on exploring the
planet. Strange things kept happening.

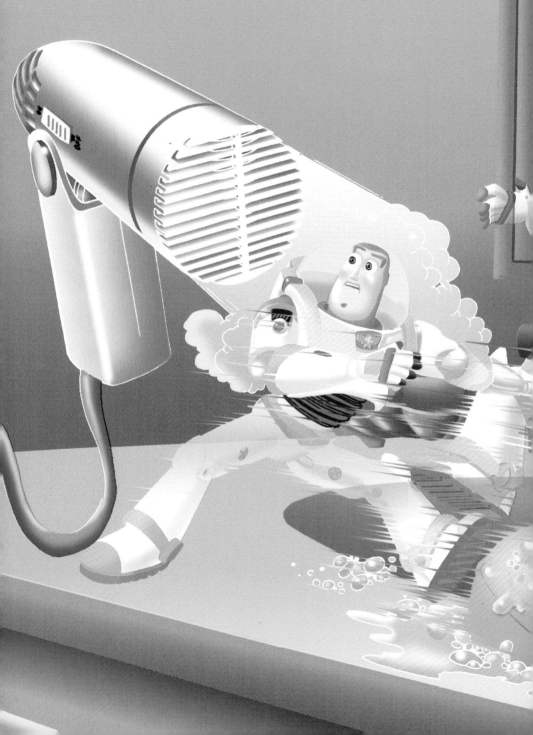

Buzz fought strong winds!

He skidded on slippery meteorites!

He was attacked by strange globs of blue slime!

Then Buzz found Andy's cat on a heap of cosmic clouds!

"The aliens here have captured Whiskers!" Buzz gasped.

He leaped in front of the cat.

"Don't worry, Whiskers!" Buzz shouted. "Buzz Lightyear to the rescue!"

"PHHHHFFFFFT!" Whiskers hissed. She flicked her tail at Buzz.

"Blastoff!" Buzz cried. He was flying through space once again.

THUMP! Buzz landed inside a bright red boat.

"This planet's surface is wobbly," Buzz said. "And so is my tummy!"

Then Buzz saw a gang of yellow creatures. They had big heads and bright orange mouths!

"Alien life-forms!" Buzz cried.

The aliens drifted over.

"Who is your leader?" Buzz called.

"Squeak!" they replied.

"What a strange name," Buzz said.

Buzz drifted away. Soon he saw a happy face and the words SQUEAKYCLEAN BUBBLES!

"You must be Squeak!" Buzz shouted.

Buzz pointed to his chest.

"I am Buzz Lightyear," he said. "I come in peace."

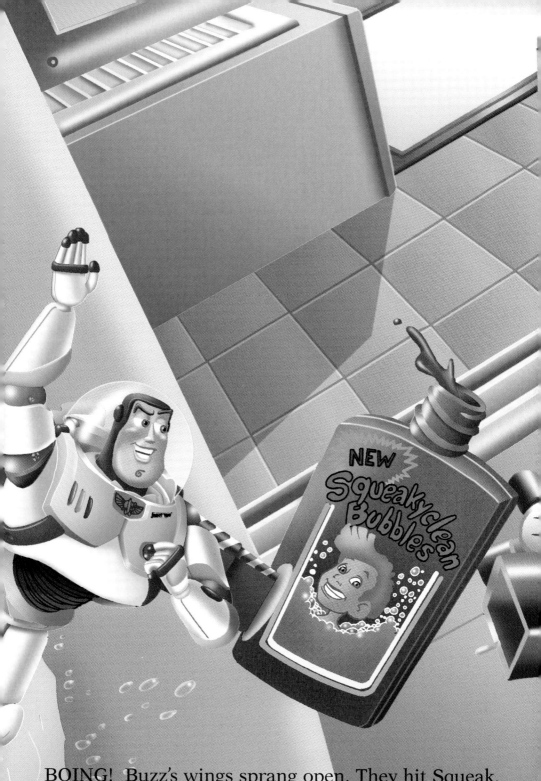

BOING! Buzz's wings sprang open. They hit Squeak.
The aliens' leader began to fall!

Buzz watched as thick pink goo poured from Squeak's head. The goo turned into hundreds and hundreds of bubbles around Buzz.

"I am under attack!" Buzz cried.

Buzz karate-chopped the air. It didn't help. The goo kept pouring. The bubbles kept coming and coming!

"Hai-yaaa!" Buzz shouted. "Back, you beastly blobs!"

Sarge and his troops were nearby.

"We have located the spaceship!" Sarge whispered into his walkie-talkie.

"Where's Buzz?" Woody asked.

"In the bathroom!" Sarge answered.

Hamm sighed. "This is a fine time for Buzz to take a bath!"

"Should we save him?" Sarge asked.

Rex looked out the window.

"Hey, Woody. Here comes Andy," Rex called. "And he looks really dirty."

Woody smiled. "Help is on the way, Sarge!"

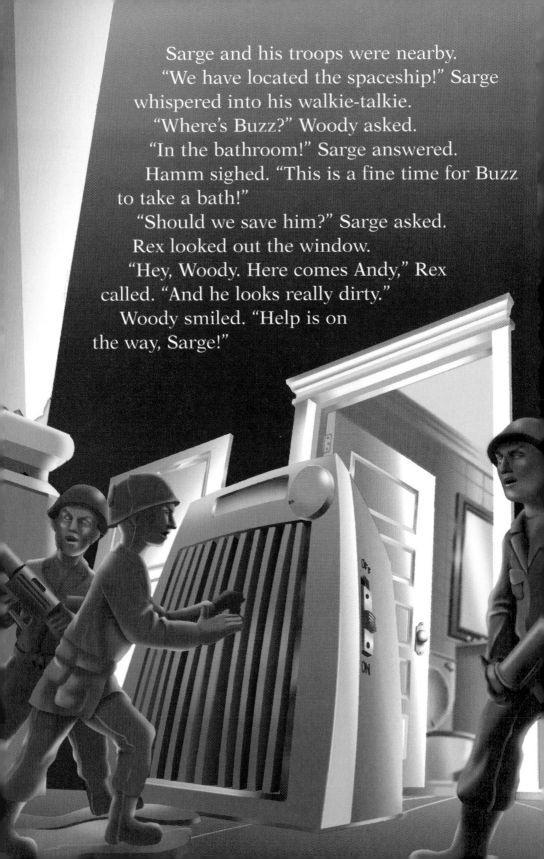

Back on the Bubble Planet, Buzz was in real trouble.
More and more bubble goo poured from Squeak. The
yellow aliens swam up to help their leader.
Aliens were all around Buzz. He was losing his hold.
Soon he would fall into Squeak's bubbly trap.

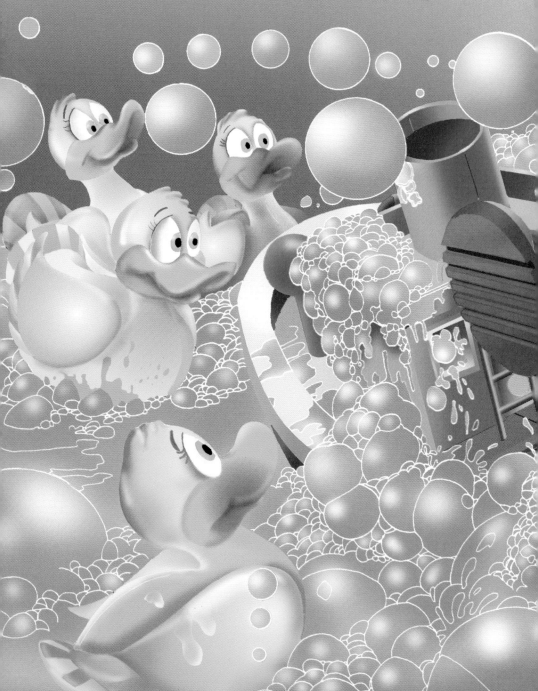

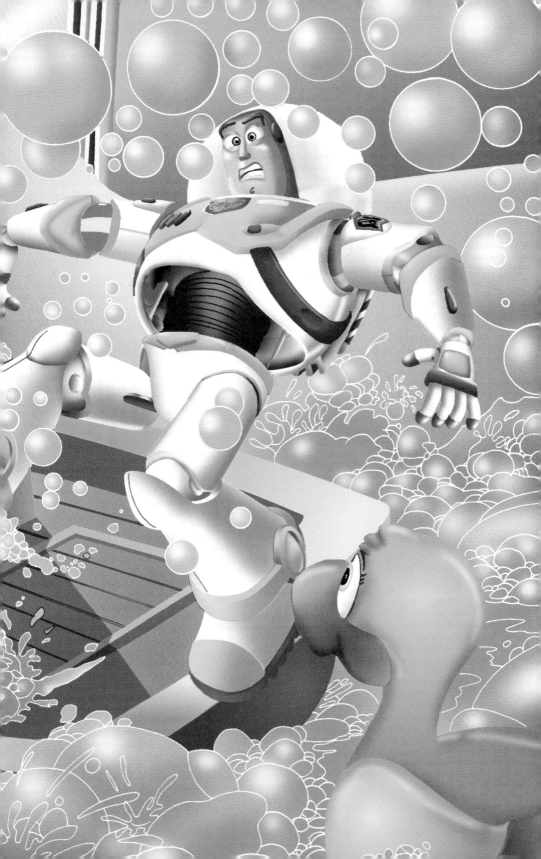

Suddenly, Buzz heard a voice he knew: "Hey! How did you get in here?"

It was Andy!

Andy lifted Buzz into the air.

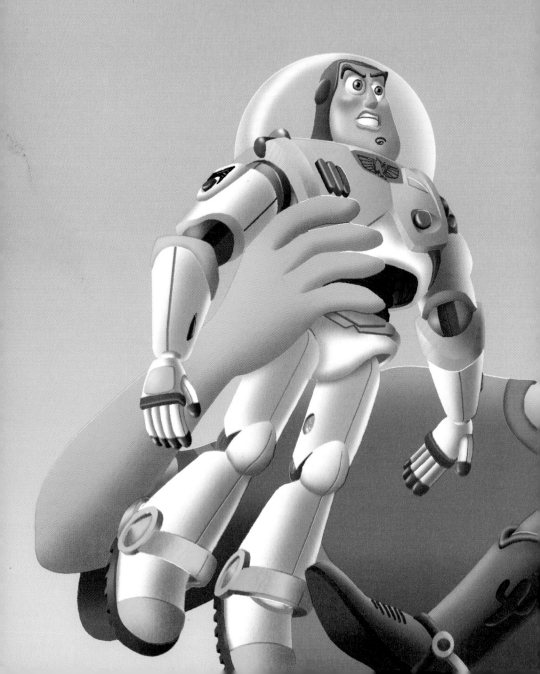

"This tub ain't big enough for the two of us," Andy said in his best cowboy voice. "But it IS big enough for the THREE of us!"

Buzz looked at his friends and smiled. He was
a lot closer to home than he had thought.
. . . And a lot cleaner, too!